STORIES THAT AWAKEN

STORIES THAT AWAKEN

TALES THAT HELP YOU SEE LIFE WITH NEW EYES

DR. PRASHANT KAKODAY AND SARAH FITZGERALD

JUPITARIAN PUBLISHING
www.jupitarian.com

Copyright © 2025 Dr. Prashant Kakoday and Sarah FitzGerald

All rights reserved.

The moral right of the authors has been asserted.

No part of this publication may be reproduced, stored in a retrieval system, or transmitted in any form or by any means—electronic, mechanical, photocopying, recording or otherwise—without prior permission in writing from the publisher, nor may it be otherwise circulated in any form of binding or cover other than that in which it is published and without a similar condition being imposed on the subsequent purchaser.

Certain tales in this collection are original adaptations of traditional or public-domain stories. The commentaries, interpretations and structure of the collection are entirely the authors' own creative work.

Published by Jupitarian Publishing

ISBN 978-1-7399466-4-7

Typesetting services by BOOKOW.COM

To BapDada — the one who turns the story of life into a Journey to the Wonderland.

Preface

As one might expect, stories don't come all at once. For us, the rich environment of knowledge was the quiet source of inspiration—and often one story would give rise to another. They arrived quietly, at different times, as reflections from moments of seeing life a little differently.

Through our experience with people from all backgrounds and ages, one thing has stood out: stories help us learn faster. An amusing observation from those who attended our talks years—or even decades—ago is that what they remember most is the story. They often share that the message within it has sustained them all this time.

Some of the stories in this collection are folk tales—simple, enduring narratives that express spiritual ideas with surprising clarity. They have helped us understand subtle concepts more easily, and we hope they offer the same support to the reader.

Each story holds a clue to something deeply familiar yet often forgotten—a way of seeing that we recognise as true. They speak of awakening, of humour, and of the dance between sense and the absurd.

Though the characters may seem many—a bird, a merchant, a traveller—they are all mirrors for the sincere seeker.

This book is not meant to be read quickly. It is best opened like a window—when the air is still, or before sleep, or after a long day when the mind is ready to listen again. Each tale may carry its own fragrance, and sometimes its meaning will unfold only later, like a seed taking root.

Even now, these stories help us make sense of the abstract. They turn intangible ideas into something more coherent and relatable. The stories have the potential to open the Skies; but even if they only help you pause, smile, or see life with gentler eyes, they have fulfilled their purpose.

Acknowledgments

With heartfelt thanks to Belinda Westcott for her intelligent insights and discrimination. We thank Jane Kay for proofreading skills, and to Judi Rich for the beautiful cover design.

To all fellow students of the Brahma Kumaris—it is always a collective process. In a quiet, unseen way, you have continually inspired us.

Contents

The Bird and the Lion	1
The Pilgrim and Dodi	5
The Professor and the Pink Sweet	9
The Woodcutter and His Axe	13
The Genie and Kutu	17
A Fishy Story	21
Danny's Toy	25
The Eagle and the Chicken Run	29
The Seagull and the Dog	33
The Singing Camel	37
The Monk and the Stone	41
The Donkey and the Two Heaps of Hay	45
The Fish and the Two Demons	49
The Man on the Cliff	53
The Queen's Necklace	57
Lloyd and His New Ball	59
The Honey Bee and the Honey Pot	63

The Eagle and the Insect	67
Nasrudin and the Expert	71
The Fish and the Ocean	73
The Clean Laundry	77
Stephan and the Squirrels	79
Yuko and the Mouse	83
Nasrudin and the Key	87
The Fox and His Shadow	91
The Boxes	95
The Guru and the Cat	99
The Lion and the Cage	101
All the World's a Stage	105
The Sinking Boat	113
The Story of Sita	123

The Bird and the Lion

A river had broken its banks, and the floodwaters were rising fast. Men, women, and animals were fleeing in all directions, searching for safety. Amidst the chaos, a bird sat on a branch, frantically flapping its wings and crying out, "Help! Help! Please, someone do something! The water is rising everywhere!"

As the panic spread, a lion passed by, calmly walking through the rising waters. Desperate, the bird called out to him, "Oh King of the Beasts, save me! The water is rising, and I'll drown! Please, help me!"

The lion looked up at the bird and simply said, "You have wings."

Discussion

This story highlights how easily we can forget our own strength and abilities, especially in times of fear or uncertainty. The bird, overwhelmed by the rising waters, panicked and called for help, even though it had wings—the problem was not even there!

Like the bird, we too can become vulnerable to the "herd instinct". We often follow the crowd, assuming that the majority must be right. In doing so, we lose sight of our own inner potential and begin to take on problems that may not even be ours.

Spiritually speaking, we are not just physical beings vulnerable to external circumstances; we are invisible actors in the grand play of life. We ourselves are totally unharmed by the story and our existence is beyond the roles we play in this material world. However, the crowd is confused. All the actors are not seeing the distinction between themselves and the roles they play. Others join the herd. We have totally forgotten our spiritual truth—the very wings that can lift us above life's challenges.

The lion's reminder to the bird, "You have wings," is a reminder for all of us to reconnect with our spiritual intellect. By using this spiritual awareness, we can rise above the confusion and panic of the world around us. Instead of getting caught up in the drama, we can remember our true potential and fly.

The Pilgrim and Dodi

Once, a renowned pilgrim was making his way to a sacred destination. One evening, he stopped to rest at the local Dharamsala, a simple shelter for travellers. Word quickly spread through the town that this wise and learned pilgrim was among them, and the townspeople eagerly requested him to share his wisdom.

The pilgrim was willing, but it happened to be his day of silence.

A man named Dodi, who had studied sign language and prided himself on his knowledge of scriptures, offered to act as the interpreter for the townspeople. He suggested that the pilgrim use sign language, and he would relay the message.

The townspeople gathered at the town hall in anticipation. The pilgrim stood before them, raised one finger, and looked at Dodi. Without hesitation, Dodi responded by raising two fingers.

The pilgrim paused thoughtfully and then raised three fingers. In reply, Dodi clenched his fist and raised it, pointing at him aggressively. The pilgrim responded by folding his arms across his chest, as a gesture of respect, thus ending the exchange. He then turned and retired to his room.

The audience, puzzled by what they had witnessed, asked Dodi what the exchange meant. Dodi, looking frustrated, said, "That pilgrim is difficult to deal with. When he raised one finger, he was blaming me by suggesting that I am number one at lying. So I responded by holding up two fingers, indicating that I would ask two people to escort him out of town. Then he showed me three fingers, accusing me of telling three lies in one day! I got even more annoyed and showed him my fist to threaten him, and he folded his arms as if to apologise."

The crowd left, still confused and somewhat disappointed.

Early next day, the pilgrim had already completed his vow of silence. A curious villager approached him and asked for the true meaning of his message, the earlier evening. The pilgrim smiled warmly and said, "Dodi is a very wise man. When I raised one finger, I was indicating the truth that there is only one God. He responded with two fingers, asking a profound question: 'What about the unmanifest and manifest aspects of God?' This was new to me, as I had never considered that perspective before. So I raised three fingers, asking him, 'What about the Trinity or Trimurti, where God is honoured in three forms?' In response, Dodi made a fist, showing me that although there may be three forms, they are unified into One. Dodi is truly wise, and he has given me much to reflect on."

Discussion

We all live in a world of sign language—not just the language of hands, but of signs and meanings. This story beautifully illustrates the role of interpretation and perspective in communication. Just as Dodi and the pilgrim had very different interpretations of the same gestures, we, too, interpret the signs around us based on the factors inside of ourselves.

By this definition, our gestures, actions, and even our speech are all forms of sign language, and how we perceive or respond to them depends on our mental and emotional states. As a result, we live in a world where meanings are often lost in a confusion of tongues. When our hearts and minds are facing the skies, we see greatness and deeper meaning in everything around us. Even the simplest things—stones, brooks, or animals—become teachers, guiding us toward higher wisdom.

However, when our inner life becomes clouded by ego, attachments, or ignorance, we interpret the same signs with a distorted lens. We may project our own issues, seeing conflict or criticism where none exists. Like Dodi, we might mistake a profound message for a personal attack, missing the wisdom right in front of us.

Ultimately, the way we interpret the world is the only factor that determines the quality of our lives. Higher knowledge and a pure heart allow us to see the deeper truths of life and the richness of the world around us, while a troubled mind creates a troubled world within itself.

The Professor and the Pink Sweet

A professor once conducted an experiment with a group of ten children. He gathered them together and gave each child a plate overflowing with a variety of delicious sweets. The children were thrilled—there was more than enough for everyone, and they even knew they could take the leftovers home.

As the children delighted in their treats, the professor returned with a single, beautifully crafted pink sweet, topped with cream. He handed it to just one child.

Instantly, the atmosphere changed. The other nine children, who had been perfectly happy moments ago, suddenly felt they were missing out. Their attention shifted entirely from the abundance on their own plates to the one pink sweet they did not have. Some sulked, others cried, and a few openly complained, despite having plenty in front of them.

The joy they had been experiencing moments before was lost—all because of the one pink sweet they did not possess.

Discussion

This story demonstrates how the ego tends to focus on what is lacking, rather than appreciating what is already present. The children, though surrounded by abundance, became discontented the moment one child received something extra.

This same dynamic plays out in adults. The ego within us is hardwired to a victim mentality. It tends to obsess over what is missing, overlooking the blessings and resources that are already available. We live in a world that constantly generates "pink sweets"—glitter and gadgets. The ego has a lots of opportunities to compare and to compete. It is the ego that feels a sense of unfairness or outright emptiness even though we may be surrounded by abundance.

Our society too encourages this mindset of always wanting more, perpetuating a cycle of dissatisfaction. We become trapped in focusing on what we lack—whether it is the latest gadget, a higher position, or the attention of someone else—and fail to see the richness we already possess.

This pattern of longing and comparison, driven by the ego, blinds us to the joy and contentment that comes from appreciating what we already have. By just understanding the absurdity of the ego, we are able to shift our focus from dissatisfaction to gratitude. In this way, we begin to break free from this cycle and start counting our blessings.

The Woodcutter and His Axe

Once upon a time, there was a young man with strong arms and a solid work ethic. Naturally, he found a job as a woodcutter in a dense forest. He was promised by the boss that if he did a good job, he would be promoted and be the head of the entire forestry department. The woodcutter was very motivated.

On his first day, the woodcutter managed to cut down an impressive twenty trees. "Not bad at all, lad!" his boss said, praising his effort. Encouraged by his success, the young woodcutter was determined to do even better the next day.

On the second day, he rose early, full of energy and motivation, eager to surpass his previous performance. But despite his best efforts, he could only cut down fifteen trees.

On the third day, even more determined, he woke up before dawn, hoping to make up for the lost ground. Yet, despite working harder than ever, he found himself cutting down even fewer trees—only twelve. By the fourth day, his tally dropped to just ten trees.

Perplexed and disheartened, he went to his boss. "I don't understand," he said, "I'm working harder and harder, but I'm getting worse results each day. What am I doing wrong?"

The boss smiled and asked, "When was the last time you took a moment to sharpen your axe?"

The woodcutter was taken aback. Sharpen my axe? I don't have time for that! I need to be out there cutting down trees!"

The boss chuckled and replied, "If you take just a few minutes to sharpen your axe, you'll work with far less effort and achieve much greater success."

Discussion

This story serves as a powerful metaphor for how we operate in life. The intellect is like the woodcutter's axe for all of us. In today's fast-paced world, many of us are so busy working hard, striving for results, that we forget to take the time to sharpen our most important tool—our intellect.

Just as a dull axe makes it harder to cut trees, a blunt intellect prevents us from thinking clearly, making wise decisions, or even understanding our true purpose. With a gross intellect, we find ourselves expending more effort, but achieving less, unable to distinguish between what is truly important and what is merely wasteful distraction.

However, if we take the time to "sharpen the axe"—to cultivate clarity through reflection, meditation, or learning—we shall approach life with a sharper intellect. This means making better decisions with less effort, gaining insight into our goals, and aligning our actions with our deeper purpose.

Just as the woodcutter needed to pause and sharpen his tool, we must create moments in our busy lives to sharpen our intellects. Taking time for introspection and meditation is not wasted time; it actually saves a lot of time and leads to greater success. By working with a clear intellect, we are more efficient, can achieve more with less waste and live with a better sense of direction and purpose.

The Genie and Kutu

There once was a farmer named Kutu who loved working in his fields. Every day, he and his wife would tend to their crops, ploughing the land, and sowing seeds with joy. One afternoon, while Kutu was working, he stumbled upon an unusual bottle half-buried in the dirt. Curious, he picked it up and examined it in his hands. It was strange and old, unlike anything he had seen before. Feeling adventurous, he opened the bottle.

Suddenly, thick smoke poured out, swirling into the air until it formed into a towering, menacing figure—a Genie! The Genie loomed over Kutu and growled, "Why have you summoned me? What work do you have for me? Give me a task!"

Startled, Kutu replied, "I didn't mean to summon you! I've nearly finished my work for the day, and I'm about to go home."

The Genie glared at him and said, "No work? Then I will eat you!"

Panicking, Kutu quickly thought of something. "Please, don't eat me!" he begged. "See that log over there? Lift it and carry it to the other side of the field."

Without hesitation, the Genie completed the task in an instant and returned, demanding, "What's next? Give me more work!"

Kutu, now growing nervous, thanked the Genie but said, "I don't have any more work for you right now."

"No work?" the Genie bellowed, "Then I will eat you!"

Thinking quickly, Kutu pointed to another log, saying, "Take that one to the end of the town." The Genie dashed off and completed the task in mere seconds. He returned immediately, once again demanding, "Give me work, or I will eat you!"

Realising he had to come up with a lasting solution, Kutu spotted an old ladder nearby and had an idea. "Here is a ladder," he said to the Genie. "Climb up and down this ladder until I tell you to stop."

The Genie, thrilled to have a task, eagerly began climbing the ladder, going up and down, fully absorbed in his new duty. Seeing that the Genie was now preoccupied, Kutu quietly left the fields and headed home, just in time for dinner.

Discussion

This story illustrates the nature of our mind. Like the Genie, our mind constantly seeks something to do. If not given a clear and purposeful task, it can become restless, creating problems for us, much like the Genie threatening to "eat" Kutu.

When the mind is idle, it becomes a playground for unhelpful thoughts, interest in lower pleasures, irrelevant worries, and distractions, that can easily overwhelm us. Just as we might keep a diary or have a clear programme for the day, we can also create a clear programme for the mind—to keep the Genie busy. By giving the mind a simple, focused task, we prevent it from becoming a problem to ourselves.

As the saying goes, "An idle mind is the devil's workshop." When we leave our mind without a clear direction, the devil wants to use it. But when we keep it engaged with a clear programme—a programme for the mind—we harness its power for good. Just as Kutu kept the Genie occupied with the ladder, we too must keep our minds busy with a clear positive tasks and knowledge based thoughts. Then the mind becomes our ally, allowing us to live more peacefully and effectively.

A Fishy Story

Once, on a calm and warm day, a man sat by the river, patiently fishing. The water was so still and clear that he could see everything beneath the surface—the fish, the bait, and the fishing line. Many fish swam near the bait, inspecting it closely, but one by one, they turned away. They could see not only the bait but also the float and the line, sensing danger.

However, one fish was not so cautious. Drawn in by the tempting bait, it bit. For a brief moment, it might have felt a surge of excitement, but that thrill was short-lived. Soon, it found itself trapped in the fisherman's net, no longer free.

Discussion

The sensible fish remained safe; the foolish one jumped at the bait, lost its freedom, and fell under the control of the fisherman. The fisherman gained power the moment the fish became attracted to the bait, deciding its fate—whether it would live or die. In pursuing the bait, the fish surrendered its freedom and fell prey to the fisherman's trap.

This serves as a metaphor for life. We lose our freedom when we are lured by the various "baits" the world offers—whether it is wealth, recognition, or fleeting pleasures.

The material world will always present the innocent Traveller with tempting distractions, but it is when he gets impressed with these external things that he becomes trapped.

When we rely on these temporary satisfactions, we hand over control to them, becoming dependent and subservient to the circumstances and objects that surround us. Our intellect, once sharp and discerning, becomes clouded, and we may not even realise what we have lost.

The happiness we experience in such moments is like the fish's brief excitement—a deception, a false sense of joy tied to the bait. True freedom is maintained when we are not deceived and remain cautious of the baits. Just like the fish that remains free experiences the vastness of the ocean, so too we discover a deeper, Supreme Reality —beyond the glittering baits and fleeting thrills of this world, where true peace and fulfilment are found.

Danny's Toy

Little Danny was visiting another family with his parents. The hosts, wanting to keep him entertained, brought out a toy for him to play with. Danny was delighted and enjoyed the toy immensely. But as time went on, he wanted more than just to play with it—he wanted to take it home.

Turning to his mother, Danny asked if he could keep the toy. His mother gently explained that the toy belonged to someone else, and he could not take it with him.

This did not sit well with Danny. Frustrated, he threw a tantrum. He cried and wailed, even though the toy was still in front of him, ready to be played with. But in his distress, he could not enjoy it anymore. When it was time to leave, Danny continued to cry all the way home, upset about the toy he could no longer have.

The toy had been right in front of him, but he did not play with the toy. He just cried.

Discussion

Danny's desire to play with the toy was natural—there is nothing wrong with enjoying something we find delightful. However, he crosses the line when instead of just enjoying the toy from someone else's home, he shifts to wanting to own it. The moment something temporary is labelled as "mine," he deceives himself. He was upset because he saw himself as a loser and that happened the moment he fixated on possessing the toy.

How different are we from Danny? Not very different—just our toys are different. As adults, our "toys" may take the form of our job, a person, a house, or our material possessions. We are the Invisible Travellers, just passing through this temporary physical world. When we begin to create attachments, we are deceived like

Danny. We then find ourselves in the mentality of a victim, seeing ourselves as potential losers and opening ourselves to unnecessary suffering.

How would a wiser Danny have acted? He would have played with the toy, enjoyed it, perhaps even invited other children to join in. When it was time to leave, he would have returned home and enjoyed the toys he had there. On days when there were no toys, he could have played with sticks and stones, and if there were none of those either, he would have simply enjoyed the quiet, for a change. Wise Danny will enjoy life.

True wisdom comes from understanding that we are just travellers in this temporary world. Like travellers, we would enjoy and appreciate each scene and situation as it comes, without becoming attached. The traveller knows that he cannot own anything and does not need to own anything. At most, he becomes a trustee of things. He lives with a sense of freedom, appreciating life without creating childish claims and bondages. By doing so, he enjoys life—one filled with appreciation, gratitude, playfulness and peace, like the wiser form of Danny.

The Eagle and the Chicken Run

Once, an eagle's egg was laid among a clutch of hens. When it hatched, the young eagle found itself in the chicken run, trying its best to fit in. It learned to scratch in the dirt, to cluck like the others, and to follow their routines. But it never quite succeeded. "What a strange hen," the others muttered. "It doesn't even scratch properly."

So the eagle tried harder and harder to become a good hen, but no matter how much it tried, it always felt awkward and unhappy.

One day, it looked up and saw a magnificent eagle soaring high above. "Wow!" it whispered. "What is that?"

The hens rushed to answer. "That is the king of birds. It dances with the clouds, crosses mountains and rivers, and rules the sky. But we are hens. We stay on the ground, scratching in the dirt, and every night we are locked in."

The young eagle listened, and continued to live as a chicken—disappointed, restless, never discovering its true nature. And in time, it died as a chicken.

The Spiritual Message

The first message from the story is that everyone underestimates themselves. All are eagles, yet they are trying hard to become good hens. They paint their feathers, wear high heels, stretch themselves tall—all in the hope of being better hens. But their truth is incomparable: they belong to the sky.

The second message is this: do not listen to the chickens. The whole crowd is caught in "chicken-thinking." They will only ever see you as one of them. The idea of an eagle exists only as a concept in their minds, not as a living reality. To discover the wonder of the sky, you must think independently and courageously.

Now, imagine the eagle goes to a chicken therapist. The therapist adjusts his glasses and says, "I don't think you are a chicken. I think you are an eagle. But perhaps you should get a second opinion."

Here lies the great question: what should the eagle do? Should it wait for proof, another opinion, more reassurance?

The truth is, the hint is already there. Each one of us has the option to spread our wings, to feel the sky for ourselves. We have the option to prove the eagle *to ourselves*. And once you have experienced that, no further proof is needed. No one can convince you that you are still a chicken.

All we need is a hint. The rest is up to us.

The Seagull and the Dog

One day, while walking through the park, I saw an unusual game unfolding. A seagull was gliding gracefully, fairly low over the open space, while on the ground a dog was chasing after it, running back and forth in playful pursuit. The seagull, with its sharp instincts, kept a careful eye on the dog, staying just out of reach. From this safe distance, the bird could enjoy the thrill of the game—enjoying the sky and the earth, while teasing the dog down below.

As I watched, I realised the seagull was very clever because it always kept a clear distance from the dog. It knew how to play with the dog without getting too close. By maintaining that distance, the seagull could enjoy both the earth and the sky. However, if the bird were to forget and fly too close, the game would change. It could easily end up caught in the jaws of the dog, losing its freedom—and with it, even its life.

Discussion

This story offers a deeper lesson for us all. The physical world is full of beauty and wonder. Every moment can be a gift to experience and enjoy, but only if we remember to keep a distance.

The seagull would lose its freedom if it got too close to the dog—and with it, a life of pain would begin. It all then depends on the sharpness of the canines. In the same way, when we inadvertently lose the safe distance, we too can become caught in life's complexities.

But how much distance is enough? The golden rule is keep a distance of "a guest" in this world—a psychological distance. A guest enjoys his visit, appreciates the beauty of the place, but never tries to own or possess it. He comes, experiences, and eventually leaves, always aware of his temporary stay.

Similarly, when we see ourselves as guests in the physical world, we are free to enjoy its beauty without getting entangled in it. This "psychological distance" allows us to experience life with a light heart, free from unnecessary entanglements. Like a guest, we can appreciate the moment, and when it is time to leave, we do so happily.

In this way, life becomes a game, a joyful experience where every moment is a gift, and we can move through it with the same playful attitude as the seagull—enjoying both the earth and the sky, when we are free and unattached.

The Singing Camel

Alice came across a camel with an extraordinary talent: the camel loved to sing, and her voice was so beautiful that many gathered at dawn to hear her melodies. The stillness of the early morning made her songs even more enchanting. However, the camel faced two challenges that often disrupted her singing.

First, there was an elephant who trumpeted loudly whenever she sang. His boisterous noise drowned out her voice, leaving her unheard. Then, there was a fearsome dragon with sharp teeth, who frequently scared the camel and those around her with his menacing presence. These constant interruptions made it hard for the camel to sing freely, and she grew frustrated, feeling that her joy was being overshadowed.

One day, while the dragon was baring his terrifying teeth as usual, something unexpected happened—his jaw fell off! To everyone's surprise, it was revealed that the dragon wasn't a dragon at all but a mask. Beneath the mask was her friend Tom, who had been pretending to be the dragon all along.

Soon after, the truth about the elephant came to light as well. It wasn't a real elephant disrupting the camel's songs—it was John, wearing an elephant costume and making all the noise. And when Alice looked more closely at the camel, she realised that it wasn't just a camel either. Beneath the mask of the singing camel was Harry, her friend, who had been playing the role all along.

Suddenly, it became clear to everyone that the entire scenario was nothing more than a playful performance. Tom, John, and Harry were good friends, acting out their roles in this elaborate drama. What had seemed like fear, conflict, and frustration turned into laughter as Alice realised the truth. There was a world of actors behind the masks, distinct from the stage and characters they played. The "drama" was, in fact, a comedy, and once everyone saw it for what it was, they could laugh and enjoy the show.

Discussion: Seeing Beyond the Drama

This story is a metaphor for life and how easily we become entangled in the "drama" of daily experiences. Like Alice, we often take this drama at face value, unaware of the deeper reality behind it.

The spiritual model teaches us that life is much like a performance on the stage of planet Earth. What we see and experience every day is part of this grand drama, but there is more to the story. Behind the scenes, there is a world of invisible actors—souls—distinct from the characters they play. These actors are part of a larger family, invisible, spiritual and real.

However, very much like Harry and the camel, most of us are so consumed by the roles we play that we forgot our true selves. We live as though the drama is our reality, living in the identities and conflicts of the characters we portray. This disconnection from our true identity is like losing everything. It is no surprise that such lives will have recurrent struggles and sorrows. It is truly a laughable situation of the human race and it is totally missed because everyone is in the same boat. Spiritual knowledge highlights this as the primary delusion of humanity today, overshadowing all other challenges.

As Shakespeare famously said, "All the world's a stage," and like the story of the singing camel, it reminds us to step back and see life for what it truly is: a performance. Being aware of the actors behind the roles allows us to live with greater understanding, detachment, and joy.

The Monk and the Stone

One day, a man came running up a mountain, frantically searching for a monk. When he finally found him, the man breathlessly said, "Stone! Stone! Where is the stone?"

The monk, confused by the man's urgency, listened as the man explained. "I had a dream last night where I saw God. God told me to come to this mountain, where I would meet a monk who would give me a stone that would make me rich forever. I left immediately to find you. So, where is this stone?"

Realising what the man was speaking about, the monk calmly pointed to a tree nearby. "Under that tree," he said, "you'll find the stone you're looking for. That will make you rich."

The man rushed over and found the stone, but it was not just any stone—it was a diamond, shining with different colours brightly in the sunlight. Overcome with excitement, the man exclaimed, "I knew it! God is truly merciful!" Without hesitation, he placed the diamond in his bag and hurried home.

A week later, the man returned to the mountain, looking troubled. He approached the monk and said, "I am possibly the richest man in the town. No one has a diamond like this—it must be worth a fortune! But since I took it, I've been having sleepless nights. I'm afraid to leave my house. I don't want visitors because I fear they might see the diamond. I feel trapped by it."

He paused, then asked the monk, "What kind of wealth do you have that allowed you to give away this diamond?"

Discussion

What was the monk's wealth? The monk possessed a far greater treasure than the diamond—he had the wealth of wisdom, and with that comes security, inner peace, happiness and contentment. These inner qualities are the ultimate riches, beyond anything material wealth can offer.

Even when people chase after diamonds, gold, or other forms of wealth, their true goal is something deeper. They believe these possessions will bring them happiness, peace, security, or fulfilment. So the real currency is something subtler. They hope to attain these subtle treasures via those temporary supports like gold or diamonds.

Since the wealth people are searching for is inner peace, love, and wisdom, a spiritual seeker aims directly for these treasures, rather than relying on external possessions to bring fulfilment.

This story highlights the difference between the wealth of wisdom and the wealth of ignorance. In ignorance, material things like diamonds appear to be the ultimate wealth, thus we get deceived. Society has built a system that values these temporary possessions, taking them for true wealth. However, such a system is fragile and eventually collapses because it is based on ignorance.

In contrast, those who possess the wealth of wisdom understand that the real treasures are within. They view the material world and its possessions as mere props in the grand theatre of life—useful in certain situations, but not wealth. Whether they have a diamond or not, they are content, for they know that their inner riches cannot be taken away.

The wealth of wisdom brings a sense of completeness, and those who possess it never feel that something is missing. They have found the true treasures that fill them, while those who chase after material wealth remain trapped in fear and dissatisfaction. When a society is based on ignorance, it is only a matter of time before the system collapses. A system, rooted in wisdom and inner peace, is what endures.

The Donkey and the Two Heaps of Hay

Once, a farmer left his hungry donkey out in a field. On one side of the donkey, there was a large heap of hay, and on the other side, an equally large heap. Both heaps were the same distance from the donkey and looked just as fresh and delicious.

The donkey stood right in the middle, torn between the two choices. He thought to himself, "The pile on the right looks good, but the one on the left seems just as tempting." Unsure of which one to eat, the donkey hesitated and spent the entire day trying to make a decision.

Night fell, and still, the donkey could not make up his mind. The next morning, he resumed his decision-making process, but by then, it was too late. Unable to decide, the donkey eventually died of starvation.

Discussion

This story illustrates the importance of decision-making power. The donkey's indecision led to his downfall, even though either choice would have been fine. Had he simply picked one heap of hay, he could have eaten his fill and moved on to the other. Let us say, for some reason the decision was wrong. Sure! He has learnt a lesson. That helps him to be wiser and make better decisions the next time. The lesson is clear: not making a decision is worse than making the "wrong" one.

Even in our lives of personal development, we are often faced with a choice of many different options or spiritual practices. It is easy to become overwhelmed by the choices and hesitate, fearing we might pick the wrong one. However, the key is to start with one practice, as each step forward opens up new opportunities.

Just like the donkey who could have started with one pile of hay and then moved to the other, we too can start with one spiritual practice, which will naturally complement the next. The important thing is to make a decision and take action. When we are indecisive, we remain stuck, unable to progress, and risk missing out on the richness of the journey itself.

Teachers and students alike should remember that it is better to begin somewhere than to remain trapped in indecision. By adopting one clear practice, we set the foundation for further growth and exploration.

The Fish and the Two Demons

In the vast ocean, a fish and his friends swam happily, enjoying every corner of their underwater world. They would race to the surface to play with the waves, dive deep to explore the seaweed, and hide among the rocks before meeting up again. The entire ocean was theirs to explore, and the fish reveled in the freedom and beauty of it all.

Watching from a distance, two demons observed the fish and their carefree lives. The smaller demon remarked to the larger one, "These fish are so happy. No one could ever make them unhappy."

The larger demon smiled and replied, "I can make them unhappy. It's easy."

Curious, the smaller demon asked, "Really? Show me."

The big demon picked up a stone and placed it in front of one of the fish. "This stone is yours," he told the fish.

Although the fish had the entire ocean to play in, the idea of owning something excited him. The stone was beautiful, with bright colours and unique shape. The fish swam around it, admiring its shine, marvelling at how it now belonged to him.

The next day, the fish became possessive. He placed signs around the stone: "No trespassing. This is a private area." But other fish, curious about the shiny object, would stop by to look. This irritated the owner fish. Sometimes, they would touch the stone, which made him angry.

As time passed, the fish spent more and more time guarding his stone. If other fish criticised its shape, he would become upset and try to smooth it out, polishing the stone until it gleamed. Yet, no matter how much he worked on the stone, he was always worrying —why did others not respect his stone? Why did they criticise it? Why did they touch it?

Meanwhile, the other fish continued enjoying the vast ocean—swimming, playing, and exploring the endless possibilities around them. But the fish with the stone was too busy sulking, worrying, and protecting his small possession to join them.

The big demon turned to the smaller one and said, "Look at the fish now. It didn't take much to turn a happy fish into a miserable one. The entire ocean is right in front of him, but he's totally miserable with his little stone."

Discussion

This story illustrates how easily we can lose sight of the vastness of life when we become attached to small, temporary things. The fish had the whole ocean to enjoy—a metaphor for the boundless opportunities and experiences available to us in life. Yet, when the demon introduced the idea of *owning* something, the fish became consumed by that one small object.

In our lives, we often get attached to material possessions, position or people—just like the fish with his stone. We become fixated on things that are temporary, defending what we "own," and in doing so, we miss out on the larger beauty and freedom around us.

The truth and the vastness of the world are always present, offering endless possibilities. But when we become attached to the temporary aspects of life—people, positions, possessions—we lose sight of the bigger picture. Like the fish, we become trapped by our own attachments, spending our time worrying and defending. Whilst we get caught in the pettiness, we miss out on the vast ocean of life's experiences.

The Man on the Cliff

One day, a young man from Ely decided to go climbing. As fate would have it, during his climb, he lost his footing and fell off a cliff. In a desperate attempt to save himself, he managed to grab hold of a branch, leaving him hanging precariously in midair. The darkness around him was thick, and panic gripped his heart.

In his terror, the young man cried out, "God, help me! Please, help!"

To his surprise, a voice answered from the darkness, "I can help you, but you must do exactly as I say. You must trust and obey me completely."

Grateful and desperate, the man quickly responded, "Yes! I'll do anything. I trust you with my life! I'll follow you without question. My life is yours forever! But save me now!"

God was impressed by the man's total devotion and surrender. He said, "Very well. Not many recognise me or trust me the way you do. I will of course, save you. For that, let go of the branch."

The man froze. Silence filled the air. His grip tightened, and after a long pause, he hesitantly asked, "Is there anyone else up there?"

No response came.

Left with no choice, trembling with fear, the young man finally decided to obey God and let go of the branch. To his astonishment, he discovered he was only inches above the ground. The branch he had clung to so desperately had never been holding him above a deadly fall—he had been safe all along.

Now that he was safe and grounded, he could return to the tree and swing on its branch. The same branch that once filled him with panic was now a source of fun and enjoyment. What made the difference? The experience of security.

Discussion

This is a metaphor for the human condition. The "branches" we cling to are the attachments we create in this temporary world—people, possessions, position, and pounds. Though we rely on these things for stability and comfort, deep down we know these supports are fleeting and unpredictable. As a result, we lead a life of subconscious panic, always aware that our "branches" could break or disappear at any moment.

True security, like the solid ground the man discovered, comes from recognising the eternal and unchanging nature of our reality beyond. When we experience this inner security, we realise that the external world, with all its uncertainties, is a play to be enjoyed.

Once we have touched this inner peace, we can return to the world of branches—still engaging with people, positions, and possessions—but with a different attitude. No longer clinging to them out of fear, we begin to interact with the world with an attitude of play.

In this state of playfulness, we perform better, live lighter, and enjoy life more. After all, do we not all perform better when we are free from fear and enjoying the game? The one who takes support of the branches is weighed down by panic and uncertainty, but the one who has found the ground moves calmly, no matter how the branches sway.

The Queen's Necklace

Once upon a time, there was a queen who owned an abundance of jewels, diamonds, and precious ornaments. Yet, among all her treasures, she cherished one particular piece above all—a stunning yellow diamond necklace. One day, to her dismay, she noticed that the necklace was missing from her jewellery box. Panicked, she called off all her royal duties and immediately began searching for it.

The entire royal household was summoned to help. Servants searched every room, from the grand halls to the stables, turning the palace upside down in search of the necklace. They spent the entire day looking, but to no avail.

Frustrated and anxious, the queen continued searching, until, at one point, she stood before a mirror—and there it was. The necklace had been around her neck the whole time. She had been wearing it all along.

Discussion

The story reflects the human condition. Like the queen, we search frantically for things we believe we have lost—whether it be happiness, peace, security, or love. We search high and low, looking for these treasures in external places, believing that something outside of us holds the key to our fulfilment.

However, just like the queen's necklace, what we seek is already within us. The feelings of happiness, love, and security that we long for are part of our true nature and experienced when awake. But we become so focused on external achievements, relationships, or material things that we forget to look inward.

Only when we finally turn our attention to our true selves, do we realise that we have everything we needed all along. The most precious treasures in life are not outside of us; they are already within us, waiting to be rediscovered.

Lloyd and His New Ball

One sunny afternoon, Lloyd and his parents went on a picnic with family friends. Lloyd brought along his brand-new ball, excited to show it off. Everyone in the picnic party wanted to entertain Lloyd. They all gathered in a circle, ready to play a game with Lloyd and his ball.

Lloyd was eager to play, but there was one condition—he did not want anyone else to touch his ball. It was as if he had labelled it "My Ball" and could not bear to share it. The group stood in a circle, ready to play, but the game could not begin because Lloyd kept the ball clutched tightly in his hands.

After a while, Lloyd hesitantly threw the ball to someone. But the moment another person touched it, Lloyd panicked, running to snatch it back, shouting, "My ball! My ball!" He returned to the circle, but now he looked at everyone suspiciously, as though they were enemies trying to steal his prized possession.

This pattern repeated several times. Lloyd would reluctantly throw the ball, but each time, he would dash to reclaim it as soon as anyone else tried to play. There was no game, only a frustrated little boy clutching his ball while everyone else stood around, unsure of what to do.

Eventually, it was time for the picnic meal. A delicious spread was served, and everyone eagerly picked up their plates. Lloyd, however, faced a dilemma: in order to eat, he would have to let go of his ball. The moment he placed the ball down to free his hands, someone else picked it up to play. Frustrated, Lloyd dropped his plate and ran to retrieve the ball. Each time he tried to return to his meal, someone else would pick it up again.

In the end, Lloyd chose to skip the meal altogether, standing off to the side, watching everyone else enjoy the picnic while he guarded his ball. Hungry and upset, he was left alone, clutching the ball and seeing everyone around him as "nasty enemies" trying to take it away.

Discussion

Lloyd's experience shows how clinging and control can rob us of joy. Lloyd could not enjoy the game, nor could he enjoy the meal, because his attachment to the ball turned everything around. He was seeing himself as a potential victim.

Now, imagine a World Cup final between France and Brazil. If the players believed they had to keep the ball for themselves, it would turn the game into a war. They then would want to claim the ball. Each player would try to tear a piece of the ball for themselves, thinking that whoever holds the biggest piece is the winner. They would forget the whole point of the game—to pass the ball, cooperate, and play together.

When players understand that the ball is meant to be shared, they begin to enjoy the spirit of the game. They pass it around, work together, and celebrate the flow of play. The game becomes not just enjoyable for the players, but for everyone watching—whether in the stadium or around the world. The joy comes from participation, teamwork, and the shared experience. The point is not to own the ball.

In the present society, it appears it to be totally normal to have a "my, my" mentality. We cling to possessions, relationships, and roles, believing they belong to us and us alone. This mindset turns life itself into a war—a constant battle to protect what we believe is ours, leaving us suspicious of others, fearful that they might take something away from us.

If we step back from this mindset, we rediscover the true "game" of life. If we learn to let go of the need to possess and instead appreciate the spirit of cooperation, we unlock a new level of enjoyment. Life becomes less about owning and more about experiencing, engaging with others, and appreciating every moment.

In this way, life becomes a joyful game, one in which not only the participants, but the whole world can take part and celebrate.

The Honey Bee and the Honey Pot

Once upon a time, there was a honey bee living joyfully in a vibrant garden. The bee spent its days playing with the gentle breeze, dancing among flowers, and gathering nectar to make honey. Life was simple, free, and full of light.

One day, while flying through the garden, the bee stumbled upon an unexpected treasure—a large honey pot, brimming with the most exquisite, refined honey it had ever seen. "This must be for me!" the bee thought excitedly, its eyes wide with delight. It eagerly dived into the pot, indulging in the sweetness that seemed endless.

At first, the bee was ecstatic. There was no need to work hard, no need to gather nectar from flowers. Everything it could ever want was right there, in abundance. But after some time, the bee began to notice something alarming—it was sinking deeper into the honey. Slowly, the sweet gift turned into a trap. Its wings became heavy with the sticky substance, and soon its nose and ears were clogged with honey. The bee struggled, its tiny body stuck, suffocating in the very thing that had once brought it so much joy.

The bee desperately tried to escape, but the more it struggled, the deeper it sank. What had once been a blessing now felt like a curse. The honey was suffocating, trapping the bee in its embrace. It was sweet, but it was also overwhelming—too much of a good thing had turned into danger.

The bee realised its most urgent need: to free itself from the honey pot, to breathe again, and to regain the use of its wings. After much effort, the bee finally managed to break free and return to the sky. The fresh air filled its lungs, and the freedom of flight returned. Now, the bee could truly enjoy the honey—not by drowning in it, but by experiencing its fragrance, appreciating its sweetness with caution and without losing itself in it.

Discussion

When we see the big map, the physical world is like a honey pot. It is all sweet and beautiful… but caution please! You can get drowned in it. This story beautifully mirrors the human experience, where life presents us with many gifts that offers initial joy and fulfilment and go a bit far, the same world can easily lead to entrapment. Just as the bee becomes stuck in the honey pot, we too are already deceived by the very things we desire—be it material wealth, comfort, or the pursuit of personal success. Often, we do not realise we are being deceived until we feel suffocated, much like the bee did.

The wise approach is to recognise the early signs of becoming trapped in the mundane and find a way out, begin to breathe again, stepping back to regain perspective. True freedom comes when, like the bee, we can enjoy life's sweetness without becoming stuck in it, appreciating the beauty of the world while maintaining our ability to fly, unbound by its temptations.

The Eagle and the Insect

The idea of higher consciousness is easily grasped through this story.

On a farm, there was an insect living on the back of a pig. While crawling along, it stumbled upon a patch of mud. Amazed, it thought to itself, what a vast and wonderful land I have discovered!

Excited, the insect got to work—building fences, putting up notices, and proudly claiming the land as its own.

Just then, an eagle swooped down and asked, "Do you want to come to the sky? Do you want to become an eagle?"

The insect hesitated. "The sky? What is there in the sky? What does it even mean?"

The eagle replied, "I will show you the world beyond the clouds … the sun, the valleys, the mountains. You will see the trees, the animals… and yes, you will even see the pig properly."

The insect was intrigued. "That sounds extraordinary… but I have just discovered this amazing land. I can't let go of it. This is something very rare."

Then, after a moment of thought, the insect added, "I would still consider coming to the sky, but come back in a week. By then, I should be free."

The eagle flew away and, as promised, returned a week later. "Do you want to come to the sky?"

The insect replied, "Actually, I have found even more land! These are extraordinary times—new opportunities! I am a success now. I can't leave at this moment. But let's try again in another week."

The eagle soared high into the sky once more, but after another week, it returned. "Are you ready? Do you want to come to the sky?"

The insect sighed, "There are cracks appearing in my land… I'm busy fixing them. In fact, I need help myself! How can I just drop everything and go to the sky? No… I'd better not even think about the sky."

And so, the insect remained in the mud, still on the back of the pig.

The Message of the Story

This story illustrates two levels of consciousness. Each of us faces the same choice: to live as the insect—caught up in its own idea of success, like an ant striving to be a bigger ant in an anthill—or as the eagle, soaring in true freedom.

The insect has its own ideas of progress and achievement, and it finds happiness in its small world. But when seen from a broader perspective, there is no comparison between the life of an eagle and the life of an insect.

An eagle would never choose to settle in the mud and call it success.

All that is required is to step out of the "successful insect syndrome".

A wise person does not compromise the sky for even a single second.

Instead, their approach is: "I want to experience the sky now. I want to be the eagle in this very moment. If there are still things to fix, cracks to repair, or others to help, I will do them as an eagle, not as an insect."

This is our story. The choice is always ours: "Do you want to come to the sky?"

Nasrudin and the Expert

Nasrudin owned a small shop where he sold various types of eggs. One day, a professor walked in the shop, and Nasrudin, with a playful glint in his eye, hid something between his two palms. He asked the professor, "Can you guess what I'm holding?"

The professor, adjusting his glasses thoughtfully, replied, "Give me a clue."

Nasrudin grinned and said, "I'll give you more than one. It's white on the outside, white and yellow inside, roundish in shape, commonly used in cooking, and has a connection with a hen."

The professor, stroking his chin, exclaimed, "Aha! I've got it—it's Dundi Khuda, an African cake!"

Discussion

This story highlights how experts miss the obvious. Nasrudin, standing in his egg shop, with all eggs round him was clearly holding an egg—something obvious to a layman. However, the professor, with all his knowledge of obscure things, overcomplicated his thinking and jumped to a far-fetched conclusion.

We often see this in scientific circles. When it comes to Paranormal experiences, the explanations offered are often overly complex, missing the obvious and straightforward truth that is right in front of everyone.

The Fish and the Ocean

Once upon a time, there was a fish that lived in a vast ocean, enjoying life swimming among other fish, both big and small, and delighting in all that the underwater world had to offer. Over time, the fish noticed the land beyond the ocean where humans lived. They seemed to be happy, playing music and having fun. Curiosity took hold of the fish, and it decided to venture out of the water to explore this unfamiliar world.

At first, life on the land was suffocating for the fish, but it adapted by using an oxygen mask. Though breathing remained difficult, the fish began trying new and expensive models of oxygen masks, convincing itself that this was progress. As the fish became more fascinated with human life, it even found itself in a nightclub one day, thinking, "A little suffocation is worth it for all this fun."

Gradually, the fish became fully absorbed in the land and forgot about its life in the ocean. However, it remained strangely drawn to images of the sea, collecting paintings and photographs of water without understanding why. Lots of time passed by! Life was hard for the fish with its oxygen masks and adjusting to suffocation all the time. One day, its friends announced, "Today, we're going to have a day out by the ocean!" The fish asked, "Ocean? What is the ocean?"

The friends persuaded the fish to join them and it returned to the ocean. As soon as it re-entered the water, the fish realised something astonishing—it could breathe naturally again, without the need for an oxygen mask. "This is beyond belief!" the fish exclaimed. There was no suffocation, only a sense of ease and belonging. The fish realised that it had been living an unnatural life on the land and that its true home was the ocean, where life was effortless and peaceful.

Discussion

This story serves as a powerful metaphor for our spiritual journey and the disconnection we all experience from our eternal incorporeal world. Like the fish in the story, we belong to a reality of natural peace, joy, and contentment—our Supreme Home. This is our original state, where we feel at ease, much like the fish in its ocean. However, as we venture into the "land" of material existence, we become distracted by the attractions of the physical world. We begin to believe that success lies in accumulating possessions or indulgent experiences, just as the fish mistook the glitter of the nightclub for progress. In doing so, we are taken further away and emotionally disconnected from our true Home. Even as the struggle and suffocation set in, we accept them as the price of modern life—convinced that this is simply how life must be.

Yet, even in the midst of this struggle, we remain drawn to memories of our original state, represented by the fish's fascination with images of water. When we reconnect with a higher consciousness and rediscover our Supreme truth, we realise that we were living unnaturally all along. This higher state of awareness brings us back to a life without struggle, where permanent peace and joy flow effortlessly. Like the fish in the story, for human beings too, the whole experience is beyond belief.

The story invites us to reflect on whether all our suffocation, discomfort, and sorrows are self-created—and how a small shift in consciousness can reconnect us with our natural, sublime way of being.

The Clean Laundry

A young couple moved into a new house. The next morning, while eating breakfast, the young woman noticed her neighbour hanging laundry outside to dry. She remarked to her husband, "That laundry isn't very clean; she doesn't know how to wash correctly. Perhaps she needs better soap. I truly don't understand why people have dirty habits." Her husband looked on silently, not saying a word.

Each time the neighbour hung out her laundry, the young woman made the same comments, criticising the cleanliness of the wash. A month later, however, the woman was surprised to see a beautifully clean wash hanging on the line. "Look," she said to her husband, "she's finally learned how to wash properly. I wonder who taught her?" Her husband quietly replied, "I got up early this morning and cleaned our windows."

Discussion

The message of this story is simple: our perception of others is often shaped by the lens through which we view the world. When our "windows" are clouded by judgment, negativity, or assumptions, what we see in others is distorted. Instead of seeing the world clearly, we project our own imperfections onto others, assuming the fault lies with them rather than within our own perspective. Only when we clean our own windows—when we clear away the mental and emotional fog or unfulfilled desires—can we see the world and the people around us with clarity and fairness. What we perceive in others is often a reflection of ourselves, it often reveals more about our own internal state than about those we are judging. It reminds us to pause and consider whether the flaws we perceive in others are, in fact, reflections of our own biases or unresolved emotions. By shifting our perspective, we can cultivate a more compassionate, understanding view of the world, free from harsh judgments.

Stephan and the Squirrels

Stephan was visiting his uncle in Seattle when his aunt and uncle decided to take him on a picnic to Mont Real, a scenic spot just a few hours' drive away. When they arrived at the mountain and set up their picnic, they quickly realised they were not alone. A lively group of squirrels had taken an interest in their meal. These bold little creatures began jumping all over the picnic table, hoping to snag some food for themselves.

Stephan's aunt, always kind-hearted, tried to appease them by offering nuts and other treats. The squirrels were relentless, darting across the table, landing on plates, and even hopping onto people's heads. It became chaotic, and the more they were fed, the bolder they seemed to become. It was like a war being fought on all sides.

Stephan decided enough was enough. With an aim to restore some order, he jumped up and began to chase the squirrels away from the table and into the nearby bushes. But the squirrels were not giving up easily. As expected each time Stephan turned his back, they would race towards the table. Stephan chased them back a couple of times. Next they would just poke their heads out of the bushes, ready to make another dash for the food. Stephan decided just to stand there for a while and each time, they would poke their head out, he would clap and chase them away. This happened a couple of times. He stood there until they finally gave up. To everyone's surprise, the squirrels had retreated for good, and the picnic could continue in peace.

Discussion

This story mirrors a deeper truth about handling challenges early on, especially when it comes to facing our own lower nature, which we call Maya. Just like Stephan needed to take action before the squirrels overwhelmed the picnic, we must address the problems we face—particularly the subtle workings of Maya—before they grow too large to manage. There is wisdom in the old saying, "A stitch in time saves nine." If we allow issues to fester beyond their early stages, we'll end up fighting a much tougher battle later.

For example, had Stephan not acted swiftly, the squirrels would have made the picnic unbearable. History offers its own lesson: had the forces of tyranny been stopped early, the Second World War might have lasted only weeks. But with every delay, the world was drawn into six years of conflict. This applies to our inner battles with Maya and negativity. If we recognise Maya—the first flicker of a troubling thought or feeling—and stop it immediately, we prevent it from spiralling into a much larger battle. When we stop these impulses early, we avoid the need for a long, drawn-out struggle.

Yuko and the Mouse

Once, in the town of Taligoa, there lived a young man named Yuko who decided to dedicate his life to spiritual pursuits and become a sannyasi, a monk. To deepen his meditation, he climbed to the summit of Mount Altino, seeking peace and solitude. However, as soon as he began his practice, a small mouse in the nearby bushes started rustling and disrupting his focus.

Frustrated, Yuko thought, "This mouse will not let me reach the depths of my meditation." Determined to solve the problem, he returned to town and brought back a cat, hoping it would keep the mouse away. Indeed, the mouse was silenced, but now the cat meowed endlessly, disturbing his practice yet again.

In search of a solution, Yuko ventured into town once more and came back with a cow, thinking that providing the cat with milk would keep it content and quiet. Finally, he believed he had found peace—he had a cat to deal with the mouse, and a cow to feed the cat.

But the farmers nearby noticed his situation and suggested, "You'll need a proper field to graze the cow. We have some spare land, and since you are a monk, we'll give it to you, but you must care for it properly."

Now, Yuko not only had a cat and a cow but also a field to manage. Still eager to pursue his meditation, he realised he could not handle all the tasks alone. Once again, he returned to the town, this time seeking a wife to help tend to the cow and field while he focused on his spiritual path.

But life with a wife brought its own challenges. She began asking for a bigger oven, and then for diamonds. Before long, Yuko found himself working a job in town just to maintain the growing demands of the life he had unwittingly created, far removed from the simple sannyasi he had set out to be.

Discussion

This story illustrates how Yuko, who initially sought a life of spiritual simplicity, ended up entangled in worldly distractions. It all began with something as small as a mouse, but gradually, one problem led to another, pulling him deeper into a web of complications.

The spiritual lesson here is that life will always present challenges—a mouse today, a cat tomorrow. These external disturbances are part of the human experience. Rather than waiting for the perfect conditions to start our spiritual journey, we must recognise that the present moment, with all its imperfections, is the ideal time to begin. Maya convinces us that we can only make progress when circumstances are just right—when the noise stops, when we are healthier, when our responsibilities lessen. But true wisdom lies in understanding that the present moment, as it is, is always the best opportunity for spiritual awakening.

Nasrudin and the Key

One evening, Nasrudin was crouched under a streetlight, searching intently for something. His neighbour noticed and approached him, asking, "What are you looking for, Nasrudin?"

"I've lost my key," Nasrudin replied. Feeling helpful, the neighbour joined him in the search.

After some time of looking without success, the neighbour asked, "Are you sure you dropped your key here?"

Nasrudin replied, "Oh no, I dropped it in the kitchen."

Surprised and a little frustrated, the neighbour exclaimed, "Then why are you looking here?"

Nasrudin calmly replied, "Because it's bright here, and the kitchen is dark."

Discussion

Nasrudin's story highlights a common human tendency—we often search for solutions or happiness where it is easy or convenient, rather than where we are truly likely to find them. Just as Nasrudin searched under the streetlight because it was easier to see, we look for peace, happiness, and security in external places because it feels easier than looking within ourselves.

Nasrudin will find the key where he lost it, not where it is easy. Where did we lose our happiness? Not in other people, because we did not even know all these smart people when we lost our peace. Certainly not in other places because we were not even aware of these beautiful places when we lost our peace.

So the answer to what we have lost—whether it is peace, love, or happiness—will not be found outside. Just like Nasrudin's key was not outside in the street, our answers are not outside of us. We did not lose our happiness in other people or in other places. So, where did we lose it?

What we have truly lost is ourselves—our true selves. The peace, love, and happiness we seek are not somewhere "out there"—they have always been within us. The challenge lies in looking in the right place, even if it is not as easy as the "well-lit" distractions of the outside world. We may need to begin the quiet journey of rediscovering ourselves. We shall then rediscover the treasures that were hidden, not lost.

The Fox and His Shadow

Early one morning, in the peaceful countryside of Cambridge, a fox was enjoying the fresh spring breeze. As he strolled through the fields, he happened to notice his shadow stretched out across the ground. To his surprise, it appeared enormous.

"Goodness!" the fox thought to himself, "I didn't realise I was so big! Now that I know how large I am, I'll need an elephant for breakfast."

Filled with newfound confidence in his size, the fox spent the entire day searching for an elephant to satisfy his hunger. But of course, there were no elephants to be found in the countryside of Cambridge. By the end of the day, the fox was exhausted, hungry, and frustrated, having chased after an impossible desire.

Discussion

Betty was a girl from a privileged background—blessed with beauty, wealth, and a loving family. She had everything one might wish for, yet Betty was constantly dissatisfied. She complained that the gifts she received were not good enough, or that she had not been invited to a certain party. Despite everyone's efforts to make her happy, her demands grew larger and more extravagant. She felt no one is as unlucky as herself.

In the same town lived a young boy named Dan. Dan had a disability that limited his physical activities, and he relied on his family for support. Despite these challenges, Dan always expressed gratitude for the life he had. His eyes sparkled with joy, and he often spoke of how wonderful life was.

The contrast between Betty and Dan raises a fundamental question: Why does someone who has so much feel unfulfilled, while someone who is severely disadvantaged remains joyful and positive.

The answer lies in the shadow. Like the fox in the story, Betty had created a large shadow of herself—an image of herself based on her wealth or the size of her house or the make of her car. The big shadow made her believe she needs an elephant. Nothing was ever good enough because the shadow was big, casting a long list of demands: bigger gifts, more respect, more love.

Just as the fox expected an elephant for breakfast, Betty's inflated shadow made her feel entitled to things. As our shadow grows, so do our demands. We might want an even bigger house, more recognition, or endless validation. These demands stem not from necessity, but from the shadow we create in our minds.

Dan, on the other hand, had a smaller shadow or perhaps none at all. Because he carried only a small shadow, he wasn't looking for an elephant. He was not driven by inflated expectations or a sense of entitlement. For him, everything was a gift—every experience was a gift, even his body, the people around him, everything appeared to him as a gift, something to appreciate rather than just demand.

The difference between Betty and Dan shows us how our perspective changes so much just by creating these shadows. What are these shadows? False "ego" acts as shadow. Just as a fox thought it was reasonable to use the image created by the shadow to define him, in the same way, when we let the things around us—a car, a career, a social image—define who we are, we step into the shadow of false ego.

It is worth experimenting with the stage without any shadows. In that state, you are not defining yourselves by anything of this world, not even the body. You are simply an invisible presence, an observer of a foreign world. A state free of shadows creates a feeling that "no one owes me anything", "the world doesn't owe me anything." Every moment will appear as a gift, just as it comes. Life will be filled with more gratitude and appreciation. It is one of the easiest ways to bring about a positive predisposition.

It is worth reflecting on why we make demands on life. We may expect certain comforts—good food, friendship, respect, or health—simply because we had them yesterday. But what justifies these expectations? Does the world owe us anything more than it does to others who may be less fortunate? Shadows creates demands and expectations and blocks us from seeing the wonder that's around us. The false ego is, at its core, the seed from which all negativity begins.

If we were to let go of our shadows, we would let go of our demands. We would discover a sense of lightness, gratitude, and wonder in everyday things. The very fact that we have a body, that we have friends, that we can experience the beauty of nature, would all be seen as gifts. The world doesn't owe us anything. When we understand this, life becomes a marvel—a source of constant appreciation, rather than a platform for endless desires, demands and disappointments.

The Boxes

Once, a grand meeting was held to discuss how to save the planet. Experts from various fields—environmentalists, climate scientists, and those passionate about protecting the Earth—gathered to share their knowledge and ideas. The room was filled with lively discussions, and the attendees were deeply absorbed in the presentations.

In the middle of the meeting, one delegate noticed some empty boxes stacked at the back of the hall. After a while, curiosity got the better of him, and he walked over to pick up one of the boxes. He was still interested in the discussions, but the allure of owning one of those little boxes distracted him. Soon, another attendee saw him take a box and decided to get one too.

Before long, the attention of the entire room shifted. One by one, people left their seats to grab a box. Some collected two, others went for the larger boxes, and a few were left empty-handed. In no time, the focus of the meeting had drifted away from saving the planet—now, everyone was consumed by the boxes.

Recognising the growing demand, Pedro started a factory to produce more boxes. Not wanting to be left behind, Manuel launched an advertising company to promote the boxes. His marketing strategies were clever—buy a blue box or a box with a sticker, and you would get a third one for free.

As interest in the boxes spread, Nikita founded a transport company to distribute and export the boxes far and wide. Soon, boxes became so valuable that Freda opened a gun manufacturing company to help protect them from being stolen. People were getting injured, hence Sanjay saw the need of medical aid and opened a hospital. Soon he was a successful Director of a very busy medical system. The boxes were in such high demand that they elected a minister to regulate the box industry and oversee production.

Pedro, Manuel, Nikita, Sanjay and Freda became famous. Their businesses boomed, and their names appeared on prestigious lists of successful entrepreneurs. Statues and portraits of them were displayed everywhere, and they were celebrated as visionaries of the box industry. Everyone was busy and consumed; many very successful and euphoric.

But amid all the success and excitement, something was missing—the essence. The meeting had been about saving the planet—yet that mission had been buried under the frenzy of box production and consumption.

Discussion

This story mirrors the journey of the human race. In our pursuit of success, material possessions, and achievements, many of us have lost sight of the true purpose behind our actions. Just like the people in the meeting, who became consumed by the allure of the boxes, we are caught up in the story—wealth, recognition, or status—and forget why we started on our path in the first place.

The story serves as a reminder of how easy it is to become distracted by worldly pursuits. We may become successful, gain fame, and accumulate possessions, but in the process, we have lost even the sense of the self and with that, our original purpose—the deeper meaning of our lives. The focus shifts to superficial gains, and without realising it, we can lose touch with what truly matters.

The question we should ask ourselves is: What was our original purpose? Are we chasing things that hold little meaning in the grand scheme of life, or are we staying true to our deeper goals and values? This story encourages us to reflect on the bigger picture, our priorities and ensure that we do not lose sight of our true purpose in the midst of lower success and distractions.

The Guru and the Cat

Once, there was a guru who performed daily worship in his household. During one of these rituals, the family's cat wandered around the place of worship, making noise and causing a distraction. To maintain the sanctity of the moment, the guru asked someone to take the cat outside and tie it to a pole in the courtyard.

The next day, at the time of worship, the cat was once again tied to the pole to avoid any disruption. This practice continued day after day.

Eventually, the guru passed away, but at the time of worship, the ritual of tying the cat to the pole continued. It became a part of the daily routine, even though no one questioned why. Even when the cat was no where to be seen, they had a team to locate the cat and bring it to the courtyard.

When the cat eventually died, the household got a new cat, not for any other reason than to continue the practice of tying it to the pole during the worship.

Discussion

This story highlights how easily rituals can take shape, and how they can become detached from their original intent over time. What began as a simple solution to a temporary problem—the cat causing a distraction—evolved into a ritual that was mindlessly repeated, even after the original reason for it no longer existed.

The lesson here is about the importance of understanding the meaning behind what we do. Without reflection, practices can become empty and routine, losing their true purpose. The story serves as a reminder to question traditions and rituals that may have lost their relevance, and to remain mindful of why we do what we do.

The Lion and the Cage

Imagine, all of a sudden, you come face to face with a lion, baring its big fangs. Instantly, you would have a certain reaction—fear, defence, and a sense of being a potential victim. You would likely see the lion as dangerous, as something to escape from or fight against. Your body would respond with the instinctive reactions of fight, flight, freeze, or faint. This would be a natural response when facing a threat that could cause harm.

Now, imagine the same lion, but this time it is safely locked in a cage. How would your reaction change? You would no longer fear the lion. Instead, you might find it amusing or even fascinating. You may even grow fond of the lion, eager to watch it, and perhaps even wanting to feed it. What changed? Only one thing: the knowledge that the lion can no longer harm you. The fear has vanished, and in its place, you feel light-hearted, maybe even affectionate.

Discussion

Let us extend this metaphor to the world we live in. When we face the world with an ego-driven consciousness, ego perceives potential harm everywhere, much like facing a lion on the loose. Ego sees itself as a victim and the world as a threatening place, full of challenges and dangers. Subconsciously, we spend our lives defending ourselves, believing that the world is inherently bad, and that we must protect ourselves from its dangers.

However, if we can step into the consciousness of a "Witness"—even for a few minutes—we can see the world from a new perspective. In this state, we become the "invisible guest" in the physical world. The guest has not created attachments or ego based on this world that is not truly their own. The invisible guest is never a victim. The Witness does not act from fear, but from the quiet responsibility of a trustee—caring for what is in front of them without becoming a victim of it. Much like a person observing the lion in the cage, you see the situation with the benevolent attitude of the noble, rather than the defensive posture of the victim. The guests know they are safe, beyond harm, and that their exit from this world is guaranteed. As such, they view the world with a sense of lightness, fun, and gratitude, finding beauty and goodness in every moment. They no longer feel threatened but instead embrace the world as a positive, enriching experience.

It is, after all, the same world. The only thing that has changed is our consciousness.

All the World's a Stage

Jack took a deep breath and gazed into the distance, as though clearly seeing what he was about to speak of. His old eyes sparkled in the firelight.

Alex looked up, catching his mood, and said, "There's something special about today's story, isn't there?"

"You're right," replied Jack. "It is a special story. It's called The Story of the Atmas."

"Is it a story we know?" asked Helen.

"Oh, yes!" said Jack. "When you hear it, you'll realise you've always known it."

And so Jack began his tale.

"Far, far away, in a world quite different from this one, there lived a race of higher beings called Atmas. These Atmas were unique because they didn't have physical bodies. They appeared as beings of light, and their world was a vast, golden sky. This sky was far beyond the ordinary one we see. It was an immense dimension, beyond time and space.

"Nothing ever changed in their world. They never experienced endings and so lived with a profound sense of security and peace. Their world was constant and complete—a beautiful and permanent reality. They had no desires or expectations, and so nothing caused them disappointment. They were free in every sense of the word—free from loss and, therefore, free from sorrow. They were entirely at peace in their home."

"What did they look like?" asked Billy.

"Let's say they looked like stars," replied Jack. "But the Atmas were also a family of actors. They didn't always stay at home. At regular intervals, they would step onto a stage to act in a play, creating a magnificent performance.

"The stage was very different from their home. While their home was timeless and subtle, the stage was solid and physical. It was called E'arth. It had limits of space, and time moved in both short and long cycles. While there was total silence in their home, the stage was a place of constant noise and chatter. There were all kinds of props for every scene, and they performed against a backdrop of mountains, rivers, and clouds."

"I think I prefer their home to the stage," commented Alex.

"Both are necessary and enjoyable in their own way," said Jack. "The stage is perfect for drama, but it's not much of a home.

"The Atmas wore masks, which they called bodies, and each mask was given a name. Some masks were male, some female; some were black, and others white. They played many different roles: heroes, villains, holy men—all had their parts to play. As more and more Atmas came from their home to join the drama, the stage became increasingly crowded. They introduced numerous subplots; on one side of the stage you might see an elegant dance, while on the other side a war was raging.

"They were so creative that every scene felt fresh and new, even though the play lasted thousands of years."

"A play that lasts for thousands of years!" exclaimed Billy in awe. "That's impressive!"

"Absolutely," said Jack. "Even as the number of actors grew to over eight billion, no two masks were ever the same. It was a perfect play, with just the right mix of comedy, tragedy, romance, horror, intrigue, violence, and dance.

"There was no separate audience. The Atmas themselves watched and enjoyed the play while acting in it. Sometimes there were special effects—snowstorms, rain, or floods. All the while, some Atmas would leave the stage while others entered. They found every scene enjoyable. They had no knowledge of sorrow, worry, or stress. They simply loved the play."

"Sounds like fun to me," said Helen.

"It was," agreed Jack, "until things began to change. You see, these higher beings had one weakness: forgetfulness." Jack's voice carried a note of regret as he continued. "Over time, they gradually forgot about their home and that they were acting in a play. They began to believe the stage was their world. Taking the play to be real, they reacted to everything with a false intensity.

Unaware of their true home, they started to feel insecure—like orphans in the ever-changing drama. Panicking, they clung to the stage's props for support, but these were temporary and insubstantial. This only deepened their insecurity. Just as they thought they had something to hold onto, it would change or slip away. This made them cling even more desperately. Forgetting they were Atmas, they began treating each other as if they were their masks. They complained about the script and blamed the creator. Feeling threatened by others on the stage, they used weapons to try and get their way, causing each other pain and sorrow. It got so bad that they even started trashing the stage. Some even planned to destroy it entirely!" Jack exclaimed.

"This sounds like our story," Billy said quietly.

Jack gave a gentle sigh and continued. "In their madness, they thought they were very clever—so clever, in fact, that they awarded each other prizes. Among them was a certain Professor Brightspark. He claimed to have the answers to everything. When the confused Atmas asked, 'Where did this stage come from?' Brightspark replied, 'I know! Many, many years ago, there was a bang, and from that bang this stage emerged.' The Atmas were impressed by his brilliance.

"Another time someone asked, 'Where did all these props come from?' And Brightspark answered, 'The stool evolved into a chair, and then the chair evolved into a table… and so on.' He always had a thousand 'facts' to back him up. Although his answers changed from time to time, Brightspark always won the most prizes. Others had different answers. For example, Holyspark claimed the stage was created by a powerful Doddspark, but Holyspark won fewer accolades."

They all laughed. Alex exclaimed, "This is sounding very familiar!"

Billy added, "Yes, I think I've studied Professor Brightspark's theories—and written essays on them!"

Jack smiled and continued. "As every scene on a stage has an end, so too did this madness. Eventually, the Atmas woke up. They remembered they were acting in a play and that their true home was a timeless reality. Believing themselves to be orphans, they realised they'd always had a home. They saw the drama for what it was—entertainment, an extra experience. They rediscovered their original security and creativity.

"They remembered the truth, best captured in Shakespeare's words:

> 'All the world's a stage,
> And all the men and women merely players;
> They have their exits and their entrances,
> And one man in his time plays many parts.' "

All fell quiet as Jack uttered these familiar words, which now seemed to hold a deeper meaning.

After a while, Alex asked, "If this is our story, what can we do to wake up?"

"We certainly won't wake up just like that!" commented Helen, deep in thought.

"But why does the stage feel so real and important?" Billy questioned.

Jack smiled enigmatically and said, "We'll understand more as the curtain rises on each new story."

The Sinking Boat

Abba Malik found himself surrounded by his eager grandchildren once again. Tom, Sam, and Laura leaned in, ready to hear the secret tale he had in store for them.

Abba Malik began, "Once upon a time, there was a ship captain who chose to overlook a minor accident he was involved in. However, about an hour later, upon returning to the lower deck, he discovered a serious leak at the thru-hull. His expert team of engineers tried to fix it without any success. The boat was now destined to sink, and no one was aware of the impending disaster.

"As the captain surveyed the main deck, he witnessed a lively celebration among the passengers. Music, singing, dancing, and laughter filled the air. The captain hesitated to make the announcement amid the joyous revelry, realising that nobody was in the mood to interrupt the party.

"Cakes were offered, baked, and consumed, and the festivities continued in full swing."

Abba Malik paused for a moment, prompting Sam to ask, "Is there a deeper meaning to this story? Does the ship represent something else?"

Abba Malik nodded, "Indeed! 'Planet Earth' is in the position of the ship. The boat is sinking, while all the passengers are engrossed in the party."

He posed two questions to his grandchildren, "Imagine you were passengers on that ship, and your friends were aboard. What would you do for them? And in that situation, what would you do for yourselves?"

Tom responded promptly, "We would all come out."

Abba Malik agreed, "Of course, you would want to save others and yourselves. Offering cakes or cushions, in this context, isn't an act of love but one of deception. To relax in a special cabin, listening to special music is not a great life, but a life of ignorance."

Laura said, "My Mummy is baking a strawberry cake this evening."

Sam inquired, "In the real world, does giving gifts to others equate to giving cakes? Does it lead to deception?"

Abba Malik affirmed, "Anything that keeps yourselves or others comfortable in the sinking boat is deceptive. Choosing comfort or feeling settled without recognising the boat's true state is ignorance and leads to sorrow."

Sam pressed further, "What does it mean to come out of the sinking boat in practice?"

Abba Malik explained, "For that, you need to see the bigger map. We can't be effective with an incomplete perspective."

Sam asked, "Is it difficult to see the bigger map?"

Abba Malik replied, "It can be difficult because the bigger map includes the visible and the invisible. Seeing the bigger picture requires the grasp of the spiritual model. With spiritual sight, one sees the complete picture, involving the visible and the invisible. Ordinarily, the boat is visible, but the real passengers themselves are invisible."

He drew a sketch illustrating, "The invisible passengers belong to the invisible home, the world beyond. The physical universe is not anyone's home; passengers are not meant to settle down in any boat! The boat is not anyone's home. Bodies are seen as merely costumes used by the invisible passengers. When we see with this model, it becomes obvious that we need to save the invisible passengers and not just the costumes."

Sam asked, "Can anything ever harm these invisible passengers?"

Laura said, "My Mummy told me that souls go to heaven after death."

Abba Malik cautioned, "The invisible passengers can create their own problems. They need to remain free and be able to jump out of the boat, but they do inadvertently tie themselves to the sinking vessel."

Laura said, "Tie themselves? That's strange!"

Abba Malik: "Every time they are having just mundane, ordinary thoughts connected with the physical world, they are dangling in the sinking boat.

"As they form new attachments to elements within the boat, they forge fresh bondages. They are then tying themselves with a knot to the sinking vessel.

"Life of addiction creates intricate double knots. Sex lust also creates double knots. It means that at the last minute, even if they realise that they need to come out, those knots become impediments to their escape. The invisible passengers are innately and naturally happy and a noble race but bondages and knots keep them dangling in the sinking boat. It becomes evident that the bondages are the only reason for sorrows."

Sam asked, "Is it possible to remain totally without any knots?"

Abba Malik shared, "An enlightened person will never be deceived. He maintains a profound awareness of what is happening to the boat. Due to the understanding of the broader map and because of spiritual sight, he remains aware of who he is and aware of the world beyond the boat. He can grapple with the experience of timelessness. He harbours a deep affection for his fellow passengers. Refusing to get tied to anything himself, he finds it completely absurd that anyone would tie himself with knots to a sinking boat."

Laura inquired, "How can one come out of the sinking boat practically?"

Abba Malik explained, "Each time he uses spiritual sight, he improves his chances of coming out." Each time he remembers the Supreme home beyond, he is coming out of the boat.

"Each time he wakes up to realise that he is the invisible passenger in the boat and in the body, that's like waking up, he comes out of the boat.

"Each time, he considers himself a guest in the physical world, a temporary trustee of everything around, trustee of the body, he is coming out of the sinking boat.

"Each time he remembers his Supreme Friend, the one who always remains free, he comes out of the boat.

"These clusters of practices are like different steps. These practices complement each other, helping passengers undo knots, each contributing to the journey towards freedom."

Sam observed, "It seems like a race against time."

Abba Malik agreed, "Indeed. Each practice increases the chances of coming out soon."

Tom asked, "What about trying to save the boat?"

Abba Malik said, "Most passengers have attention on saving the boat, and more will join the task force, which is great! But there is a bigger issue of confusion. Even in smooth-sailing boats, we don't want passengers tied with knots. Ordinarily, it would be obvious for passengers to urgently step out of a boat that's in danger. But for the passengers who believe the boat to be their home, this is a confusion. They then just run in circles, wasting their precious time. Those who are free from confusion and free from knots are useful to themselves and useful for others."

Sam said, "I like to be an optimist and want to believe that the ship won't sink."

Abba Malik replied, "In the present situation, we need to start with a clear diagnosis. When we approach a crisis with an incomplete map, inappropriate sight and no diagnosis, optimism is empty—

there are more chances of being deceived or regrets later on. When an individual is sensible and the diagnosis is clear, he becomes a realist. He will get results. A realist doesn't face loss or regrets."

Abba Malik continued, "But even if one succeeds in becoming free of knots, the mission isn't over yet. Imagine you successfully emerge from the sinking boat, having diligently followed the prescribed method and became free from the knots and bondages. As you meet your Supreme Friend, he congratulates you for being free before it was too late. By now, you are experiencing that silent bliss and the relief of being free. However, the unexpected follows—your Supreme Friend instructs you to return to the same sinking boat."

Laura exclaimed, "Why? That's dangerous!"

Abba Malik continued, "You are told that your fellow passengers are still in severe danger in that sinking boat. With your firsthand experience of becoming free, you are the right person to guide others towards safety. You are told 'Go back on the same boat, utilise your time and resources for the mission but stay near the exit.' When the final whistle blows, you should be ever ready to fly back.

"You now return to the same sinking boat but with a noble attitude of an incarnate. Having gained freedom from the physical world, the invisible traveler is sent back to the same world, the same town, the same family, the same body, and the same job but with a divinised spirit. Your attitude is that of a trustee of everything, including the body. Nothing in the boat can belong to any passengers. As an incarnate, your mission is clear—to facilitate the freedom and the safety of the other fellow passengers."

Sam asked, "How does he manage life? For example, will he be doing any job?"

Abba Malik explained, "If he engages in any job, it will be for the livelihood of the body and to support his higher task. He is conscious of his real job, his secret mission. Even while eating food, his perspective is that he is providing to the body, enabling it to be used for the mission.

The Supreme friend imparts two cautions. Firstly, stay close to the exit. Secondly, do not join the party."

Laura wondered, "What eventually happens to the boat and the passengers?"

Abba Malik concluded, "The story of the visible and the invisible continues, right now, just in front of us. I see the delivery of rescue ropes, and I can also smell the aroma of freshly baked cakes. The rescue and the party will continue until the very end."

The Story of Sita

Billy, Helen, and Alex gathered eagerly around Jack, waiting for his next story. Jack closed his eyes, as if stepping into another world, and then slowly began his tale.

"In a kingdom, not so long ago and not so far away, there lived a very beautiful queen called Sita. Everyone loved Sita. She was cheerful, kind-hearted, and virtuous, naturally contented. She treated everyone equally, with a simplicity that belied her royal status. Although she was a queen, she was unassuming and approachable, forming genuine connections with all she met.

"Sita was married to King Ram, the ruler of the kingdom. Ram was the perfect king—wise, powerful, and universally admired. His subjects loved him deeply, and he governed with fairness and integrity. Simply looking at King Ram and Queen Sita, people often felt that they were not of this earth, but from another world entirely."

"Are Sita and Ram Atmas, or higher beings?" asked Helen.

"A good question!" replied Jack, clearly pleased with the attentiveness of his audience. "Sita does indeed represent the Atmas."

"And Ram?" Alex enquired.

"Ram," Jack explained, "is the name for God."

He continued, "In Ram's kingdom, there was always a festive atmosphere. It was quite unique—no one ever experienced sorrow there. It was a kingdom of constant happiness.

"However, lurking in the shadows of this perfect kingdom was an evil demon called Ravan." Jack went on, "As you may know, demons find pleasure in causing sorrow and pain to others. Ravan, the king of the demons, was ruthlessly cruel. He delighted in devising new ways to bring suffering and distress.

"Ravan hated to see Sita living such a perfect, contented life. The sight of her peace and happiness drove him mad. He resolved to kidnap her and make her his slave. That way, he would have endless opportunities to torment her. However, Sita could not be easily taken, for a protective boundary was drawn around her residence. As long as she remained within that boundary, Ravan could not touch her."

"What does the boundary represent?" Helen asked with curiosity. "And who drew it?"

Jack explained, "The line symbolises where clarity ends, and confusion begins. Let's call it 'the line of confusion.'"

"What sort of confusion?" Billy wanted to know.

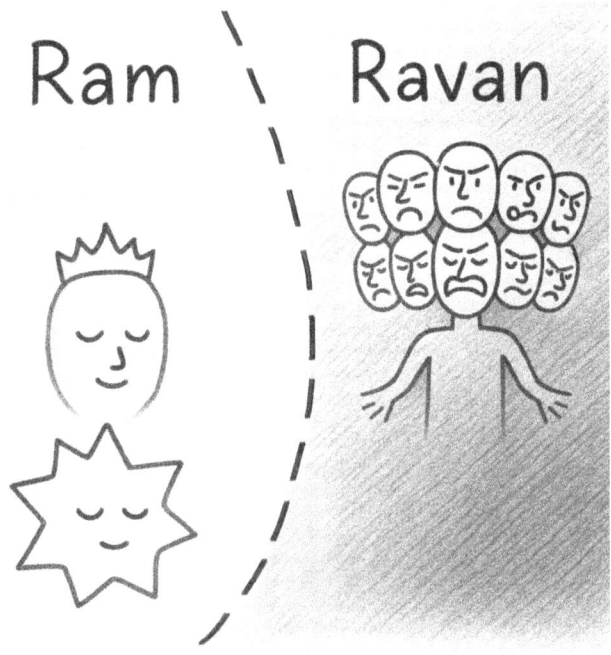

"Well," Jack replied, "Imagine someone believing they own a cloud. That person has crossed the line. And if they then start to believe they are a donkey, we can safely say they've gone far beyond it! These are obvious examples, but many times we cross the line without realising it. When we do, we lose clarity and discrimination and enter a state of ignorance.

"When a whole group crosses the line, everyone is confused—but no one notices, because they are all in the same state. It becomes a realm of ignorance, stupidity, and madness. And yet, those in it consider themselves to be very clever."

"Like Professor Brightspark!" declared Helen.

"Exactly! They're under a spell of Ravan that prevents them from seeing their own ignorance," Jack said.

"Ravan is cruel and represents ignorance, but he is also cunning. He uses his perverted cleverness to lure Sita across the line. Disguised as a beggar, he tries to win her sympathy. Another time, he sends a beautiful golden deer to tempt her curiosity. But both the beggar and the deer remain outside the line.

"Sita feels her life is perfect. She has everything she needs, and, best of all, she has Ram. But she begins to think, 'A golden deer would be nice to have. It wouldn't do any harm.' This small attraction grows into a passion until she becomes obsessed with having it. Finally, unable to resist any longer, she steps across the line to reach the deer.

"At first, Sita feels great excitement and happiness with the golden deer. But she soon discovers it was a trick. Beneath its golden exterior is a demon from Ravan's kingdom. Once she crosses the line, Ravan grabs her and takes her away."

"Does the golden deer represent our attraction to things like food and money?" asked Alex.

"Yes, it represents our attraction to anything limited or worldly," Jack explained. "These attachments cloud Sita's discrimination. Beyond the line, clarity fades, and mistakes follow."

Jack's tone grew more serious. "Sita finds herself in Ravan's kingdom, a slave to the demon king. To her horror, she learns that Ravan is no ordinary monster. He has ten heads, and she is now enslaved to all of them.

"Each head represents a different desire. One head might demand cigarettes, so Sita has to run to buy some. When that head gets its 'food,' it grows larger and demands more. If Sita isn't fast enough, it throws tantrums and harasses her. And there are nine other heads, all making demands!"

"What do the other heads want?" Jack asked, looking at them.

"Sweets!" "Fame!" "Alcohol!" "Money!" the children shouted.

"Exactly," Jack said. "Each head represents a different desire. And what lies behind all desires?"

"Our ego?" ventured Alex.

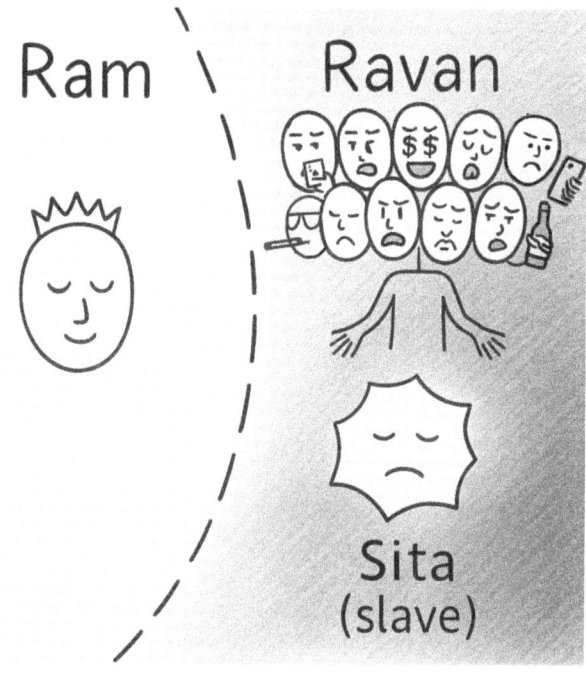

"Yes," Jack confirmed. "Ravan's heads represent the ego in its many forms. Behind every limited desire and pleasure is a head of Ravan demanding to be served.

"These heads even compete with each other to control Sita. She is kept constantly busy trying to please her master. She runs faster and faster, but no matter how hard she tries, Ravan always wants more. His ultimate goal is to cause her sorrow. Even the golden deer he offered was nothing more than a deception."

Billy, who had been listening intently, suddenly asked, "So when we kill animals for food or drink alcohol, is that because of Ravan?"

Jack smiled gently. "Yes. Ravan has no mercy and no love. He knows only his desires and addictions. But remember, Ravan can never truly harm Sita. She is immortal, invincible, and eternally safe. It is only under his spell that she forgets this and allows herself to be frightened."

Jack paused to let the weight of his words settle.

Jack's voice softened as he resumed. "So, Sita finds herself in this unfortunate state—far from her world of peace, far from Ram. She feels trapped in Ravan's kingdom, overwhelmed by his demands and the constant chaos around her.

"Ram, however, is forever wise. He never crosses the line and remains beyond Ravan's clutches. From his position of clarity, he sees Sita's predicament and sends her a message. He tells her that he can free her from this unhappy state. 'Although Ravan may seem powerful,' Ram says, 'I am almighty. I can defeat him with ease and bring you home.' His love for her is eternal, selfless, and pure.

"However, Ram sets a condition for her release. What do you think this condition might be?" Jack leaned forward slightly, his gaze fixed on his listeners.

"That she should not go back to Ravan?" suggested Alex hesitantly. "Or that she should never cross the line again?"

Jack smiled and shook his head. "The condition is simple: Sita must take the first step towards freedom. She must make the decision to leave. Ram explains to her that while his love is constant, he cannot impose freedom upon her. The choice is hers—she can remain Ravan's slave or return to being Ram's queen.

" 'If you take even one step,' Ram promises, 'I will take a thousand steps to help you.' But he will not interfere with her choice. After all, if Sita chooses to stay with Ravan, who is Ram to decide for her?"

Jack paused, allowing his words to settle. Then he asked, "Is the decision easy for Sita?"

"Yes!" the children chorused.

Jack laughed lightly. "In fact, it isn't. There is another demon in Ravan's administration—Maya. Maya's job is to befriend Sita and keep her from leaving. She is clever, cunning, and ruthlessly loyal to Ravan. She pretends to be kind and friendly, gaining Sita's trust. Maya's sole purpose is to confuse Sita and prevent her from making the decision to leave.

"Maya whispers words of doubt and hesitation: 'It's too difficult.' 'Do it later.' 'Why bother?' She invents countless excuses to keep Sita trapped. Even when Sita decides to stop feeding Ravan's heads —perhaps by giving up cigarettes—Maya intervenes. 'That's a good decision,' she says sweetly, 'but start from next month.' Sita, trusting her 'friend,' agrees. By the time the next month arrives, Sita has forgotten, or something else has distracted her.

"Maya is relentless. If Sita remains determined, Maya whispers, 'You tried before and failed. You're too weak.' Or she might say, 'Just try this harmless alternative.' In this way, Maya wins the round, keeping Sita bound to Ravan."

Helen frowned. "So Maya's job is to keep Sita from making the decision?"

"Exactly," Jack confirmed. "Maya creates doubt and hesitation, keeping Sita distracted with more golden deers or excuses. Maya's cleverness lies in her sweet, kind outer form. But make no mistake —her loyalty is to Ravan, and her goal is to keep Sita enslaved."

Sanjeevani

The next evening, Jack returned to the room, his figure casting a long shadow on the wall. His students looked up expectantly. Without a word, he settled into his chair. After a few moments of silence, he began to speak.

"In the story, there is a word—*raaz*. It means 'a secret game.' This game is taking place in everyone's head. On one side are Ravan and Maya; on the other are Sita and Ram. The task of Ravan and Maya is to defeat Sita, while the task of Sita, with Ram's help, is to win.

"Ravan and Maya are determined players. They have no mercy for their opponent. If Sita is weak, they score as many points as they can. In Sita's team, Ram is a strong player—but for the team to succeed, Sita must become strong too."

Jack's eyes swept over his audience. "In every game, winners receive prizes and losers face penalties. Those who win against Ravan and Maya experience happiness and peace, while those who lose face sorrow and difficulties. If we look around the world and see misery, it is because the game was lost to Maya."

He paused before continuing. "The progress of this inner game determines our external reality—our physical, social, and economic fortunes or misfortunes. Even the physical world itself exists within the context of this game. It may be a game, but it is one that matters deeply."

Billy, thoughtful, asked, "We're all playing this game, aren't we?"

"Indeed," Jack replied. "And in some games, like boxing, there is a result called a 'knockout.' If a player is careless, the opposition can render them unconscious. An unconscious player doesn't even realise a game is being played. In the same way, if Sita falls into unconsciousness, she forgets the game entirely. She may still be running around, but she has no awareness of what's really happening."

Helen's brow furrowed. "If Sita is unconscious, how can she possibly win?"

Jack nodded. "In the story, there is a herb called *Sanjeevani*. This mythical herb has the power to revive the dead. In this context, Sanjeevani represents the ultimate spiritual knowledge—the knowledge that comes from Ram. It is this knowledge that can awaken Sita, making her conscious again and aware of the game."

He leaned forward, his voice steady. "Once Sita wakes up, the game becomes hers to play. Sanjeevani gives her the chance to win. Without it, her chances are slim, because she doesn't even recognise her enemy—or that she is working for him. Ram's role is to give her the Sanjeevani of knowledge, awakening her to her true self, her true friend, and the reality of Ravan's deceit."

The Strategy for Victory

"So," Alex asked eagerly, "if Sita wakes up, what's her strategy for defeating Ravan?"

Jack smiled. "Sita's victory depends on her recognising one crucial fact: Ravan's strength comes from her. Every head of Ravan is fed by Sita herself. His very existence depends on her resources—her time, energy, and thoughts. When Sita is unconscious, she unknowingly becomes her own worst enemy, supplying Ravan with everything he needs to thrive.

"If Sita decides to stop feeding him, Ravan weakens with every passing moment. He may throw tantrums to scare her, but he is, in truth, a paper tiger. He only appears powerful because of the nourishment he receives from Sita."

The Strategy for Victory (Continued)

Jack continued, his voice calm but firm. "To defeat Ravan, Sita must first understand the nature of his supply chain. What does she provide to keep him strong? Her treasures—her mind, body, senses, wealth, and time. These are Sita's most precious resources, and she is their sole custodian. No one else can use them unless she allows it.

"But when Sita is confused or unconscious, she unknowingly uses these treasures to feed the different heads of Ravan. For example, her wealth—money and possessions—might be spent to satisfy one head's desire for luxury, another's for indulgent food, or another's for status symbols. Similarly, her mind might be consumed with fantasies or unnecessary worries, feeding the heads that thrive on mental distractions."

Billy nodded, his face serious. "So, Ravan's heads are all the desires and attachments we have?"

"Yes," Jack said. "Each head represents a different desire, driven by ego. Some are obvious—lust, greed, anger—but others are subtler, such as the need for approval or attachment to roles and relationships. For example, a parent might think, 'I want my child to be the best in their class.' While this seems like love, it sometimes stems from a hidden desire for reflected glory. Ravan thrives on such hidden motives, disguising them as virtues."

Jack looked at Helen, Alex, and Billy in turn. "And then there are the senses. Ravan uses them to trap Sita with pleasures of the body—taste, touch, sights, sounds. The head of indulgence might demand rich foods, even when they harm the body. The head of vanity might demand attention or admiration. Each head grows stronger as Sita tries to satisfy its demands."

Helen frowned. "But what about the mind? How does Ravan use that?"

Jack's expression turned grave. "The mind is Ravan's most fertile ground. Even when Sita refuses to feed Ravan with physical resources, he can still command her thoughts. Fantasy, regret, anxiety, and memories—these are all tools Ravan uses to keep her enslaved. When Sita replays past experiences or imagines future ones, she is unwittingly nourishing Ravan's heads. And the heads compete fiercely for her attention, creating a storm of thoughts that exhaust her."

The Turning Point

"So, how does Sita break free?" Alex asked.

Jack's eyes gleamed. "The first step is awareness. Once Sita wakes up, she realises she has the power to cut off Ravan's supplies. She decides, 'I will no longer feed these heads.' Ravan may throw tantrums to intimidate her, but every day that she refuses him, he grows weaker.

"This is the minimum effort required of Sita: to stop the supply. But there's more. Sita must not simply starve Ravan; she must redirect her treasures towards Ram. By keeping her mind, body, and resources engaged in Ram's task, she ensures they are used for her liberation, not her enslavement."

"What is Ram's task?" Helen asked.

"Ram's task," Jack said, "is to free all the Sitas from Ravan's clutches. It's a vast mission. When Sita uses her treasures to think of Ram, to reflect on his knowledge, and to work towards his goals, she becomes part of this divine effort.

"This is why Sita cannot afford to let her mind remain idle. An idle mind is Ravan's playground. But a mind filled with thoughts of Ram is safe—it becomes a fortress of clarity."

The Battle Plan

Billy leaned forward, his curiosity piqued. "What happens if Ravan tries to trick her again? Can she really win?"

Jack nodded. "Victory is not only possible—it's inevitable if Sita stays vigilant. The key is to remain awake. An awakened Sita cannot be deceived because she recognises Ravan's tricks for what they are.

"She also knows that some heads of Ravan are stronger than others. One head might represent an addiction, such as alcohol or smoking. Another might represent attachment—to a person, a role, or an image of oneself. Another head represents sex-lust—an addiction that disguises itself as love but drains the soul of purity and peace. The intelligent strategy is to tackle the biggest head first. If Sita leaves it unchecked, it will create mischief and invite others back. But if she confronts it with courage and determination, it can be starved into submission."

Jack paused, then added, "This doesn't mean battling thoughts endlessly. A wise Sita doesn't fight Ravan directly. Instead, she creates an environment of clarity by filling her mind with Ram's knowledge and presence. This clarity weakens Ravan automatically."

The Power of Choice

Helen raised a hand, her brow furrowed. "But isn't it hard to stop certain thoughts? What if they keep coming back?"

Jack smiled gently. "It's natural for thoughts to arise. The key is not to let one thought lead to another. For instance, if Sita sees an image or hears something that triggers a thought, she must stop it at the first thought. Allowing it to grow into a chain of thoughts is her choice—and that's what Ravan relies on.

"There's a saying in one scripture: 'If a man sees a woman and looks away, it's not a sin. But if he turns back for a second glance, that is.' The first thought is instinctive; the second is deliberate. An awakened Sita will not allow the first thought to lead to a second."

Helen nodded slowly. "So, she has to break the chain before it starts?"

"Exactly," Jack said. "By doing this, she denies Ravan his nourishment. And as Ravan weakens, Sita's peace grows. She experiences the liberation of being free from his demands. Each victory—each head of Ravan that disappears—brings her closer to clarity and joy."

The Role of Ram

Jack's tone softened. "Sita's success depends not only on her vigilance but also on her connection with Ram. Thinking of Ram is easy because he is supremely attractive. His unique quality is his constant happiness. No one can give him sorrow because he is fearless and selfless. He knows he is eternally safe and unchanging, which gives him complete peace.

"Because he has no desires, he loves without condition. His supreme peace allows him to elevate everyone around him. Ram's life is about giving happiness, while Ravan's is about taking it."

"What a contrast!" Helen exclaimed. "I know who I'd choose as my companion!"

Jack smiled. "And Sita knows Ram too—consciously or subconsciously. She only needs to create time to remind herself of her supreme friend. Ravan cannot use a mind that is busy with thoughts of Ram."

The Path to Freedom

Jack leaned forward, his voice filled with conviction. "For Sita to win, she must use the powers she already possesses—powers she may have forgotten.

"First, the power of decision. Sita must decide to stop feeding Ravan and step towards freedom.

"Second, the power of discrimination. She must recognise Maya's tricks and identify Ravan's heads.

"Third, the power of determination. A determined Sita cannot be defeated. If she is resolute, Ravan will not even wage a battle—he knows he will lose.

"Fourth, the power of dedication. Sita must dedicate her resources to Ram's task and remain loyal to her higher purpose.

"Finally, the power of discipline. Like any successful army, Sita must be disciplined in her thoughts, actions, and use of time."

The Ultimate Victory

"Ram's message to Sita is this: 'Win this game and help others win too. Share the Sanjeevani of knowledge. Awaken all the Sitas.'

"However, Maya's greatest success lies in creating division. In a state of ignorance, one Sita might fight another, mistaking her as an enemy. But in clarity, Sita realises that all others—regardless of their culture, country, or beliefs—are her brothers and sisters. Together, they share the same goal: to be free from Ravan."

Alex, his voice tinged with hope, asked, "Can there really be a happy ending for us humans? Even after all the mistakes we've made?"

Jack smiled warmly. "Not so much an ending as a continuation. Just as the Atmas in the first story woke up and remembered who they were, so too can all Sitas win this game. By staying in clarity, they can experience the bliss of being free from Ravan's heads. This freedom will transform their lives, bringing peace, harmony, and love—not only with Ram but also with each other."

Jack looked at his students. Helen, Alex, and Billy sat in silence, their expressions reflective. Jack could see the beginnings of deep contemplation on their faces. He knew it would be many days before their questions subsided, but he was pleased. The soul-searching had begun.

About the Authors

Dr Prashant Kakoday

Dr Prashant Kakoday is a medical doctor based in Cambridge with a background in ENT surgery and Integrated Health. For over 40 years, he has explored the riddle of human consciousness, travelling widely and speaking on spirituality, health, and the nature of the mind in many countries, including through the Accredited Medical Teaching Program in the USA.

Sarah FitzGerald

Sarah FitzGerald, originally from Cambridge, trained as an interior designer and worked at the Science Museum and several London consultancies before her journey turned inward. While teaching languages in South-East Asia, she encountered Raja Yoga and discovered what she now calls *the real interior design*—the art of transforming the inner world.

The authors can be contacted via the publisher's website at: **info@jupitarian.com**.

www.ingramcontent.com/pod-product-compliance
Ingram Content Group UK Ltd.
Pitfield, Milton Keynes, MK11 3LW, UK
UKHW050142271125
465400UK00003B/35